A First-Start Easy Reader

This easy reader contains only 44 different words,
repeated often to help the young reader develop
word recognition and interest in reading.

Basic word list for *Muffy and Fluffy*

alike	little	the
and	look	then
are	low	there
but	Muffy	they
do	no	think
down	not	this
dress	now	turns
Fluffy	out	twins
fun	play	two
here	plays	up
high	says	wait
if	sometimes	we
in	take	will
is	talk	yes
kittens	that	

Muffy
and Fluffy

The Kittens Who Didn't Agree

Written by Janet Craig

Illustrated by Susan Hall

Troll Associates

Library of Congress Cataloging in Publication Data

    Muffy and Fluffy.

    (A First-start easy reader)
    Summary: Muffy and Fluffy, twin kittens who do not
think alike, have trouble agreeing on anything until
they discover that it is fun to take turns making
choices.
    [1. Twins—Fiction. 2. Cats—Fiction] I. Hall,
Susan, 1940-   ill. II. Title. III. Series.
PZ7.P1762Mu   1988   [E]   87-16227
ISBN 0-8167-1227-1 (lib. bdg.)
ISBN 0-8167-1228-X (pbk.)

Muffy and
Fluffy are
twins!

This is Muffy.

And this is Fluffy.

Muffy and Fluffy look alike.

They dress alike.

They talk alike.

They are twins.

But Muffy and Fluffy
do *not* think alike.

If Muffy says *yes*—

Fluffy says *no*.

If Fluffy plays in—

Muffy plays out.

If Muffy plays high—

Fluffy plays low.

If Fluffy plays up—

Muffy plays down.

The two little kittens
do not think alike.

And that is *not* fun!

"We will play here," says Muffy.

"No," says Fluffy.

"We will play there."

"Wait," says Fluffy.

"We will take turns."

"We will play here."

The twins play here.

Then they play there.

They play in . . .

and out . . .

high . . .

and low . . .

up . . . and down.

"This is fun!" says Fluffy.

"Yes," says Muffy. "This is fun!"

Now Muffy and Fluffy look alike.

They dress alike.

They talk alike.

Sometimes the twins

do *not* think alike.

And sometimes they do!